SNAKE KING
of the Kalinago

A CIP catalogue record for this book is available from the British Library.

Printed in China
Design by Andy Dark

ISBN: 978-0-9532224-6-9

Papillote Press
23 Rozel Road
London SW4 0EY
United Kingdom
www.papillotepress.co.uk
and Trafalgar, Dominica

ACKNOWLEDGEMENTS

The publisher would like to thank: in Dominica, Jamie Sorhaindo for co-ordinating the project so efficiently; Chris Lawrence for her workshop training and literacy wisdom; Micheline Bruno, teacher at Atkinson School, for her ability to coax the words out of her Grade 6 students; Alice Laurent, headteacher of Atkinson School, for her kind permission to allow her pupils to contribute to this book, and, of course, the pupils themselves who worked so hard and creatively to give us their own version of this Kalinago myth.

In the UK, in the London borough of Wandsworth, Kathy Casimir MacLean, head of the ethnic minority achievement service, and Karen Mears, ethnic minority achievement adviser, provided ideas, expertise and enthusiastic support from start to finish. The children and staff of John Burns Primary School and St Georges Primary School, both in Battersea, London, offered helpful comments, as did Aramidé Babalola.

Papillote Press is also grateful to Mary Walters, editor of *Yet We Survive: the Kalinago People of Dominica – Our Lives in Words and Pictures*, for permission to reproduce the paintings in this book, which were created by members of the Carib Territory Communications Group and first appeared in the original version of *Yet We Survive*, with words by Miranda Langlais.

Grade 6 of Atkinson School, Bataka, Dominica

Nian Auguiste
Dahlia Bruno
Layla Calme
Malcolm Cyrille
Shervon Dorsette
Salim Dupigny
Tyron Dupigny
Nikisha Graham
Taewa Joseph
Renie Kaufman
Jason LaRonde
Daniel Laurent
Luchiano Morancie
Nicole Paris
Romaine Paris
Endura Thomas
Shermiah Tyson
Anton Viville
Jean Viville
Alex Auguiste (absent)

with their teacher,
Mrs Micheline Bruno

About this book

The Kalinago people live in the Commonwealth of Dominica in the eastern Caribbean. They were the island's first inhabitants and arrived in their canoes from South America many hundreds of miles away. The Kalinago (also known as Caribs) were farmers and fishermen but, after Europeans arrived more than 500 years ago, they gradually lost their land. Now they live by the sea in a mountainous and rainforested part of the island known as the Carib Territory.

The Snake King of the Kalinago is adapted from a traditional myth. Like all myths, it has been changed in the telling – and the story in this book is the latest version, thanks to the children of Atkinson School in Dominica, who wrote the words.

Some of the children are from the Kalinago community and live in the Carib Territory. They wrote the text using both their own knowledge of the traditional story and their imaginations. Some ideas also come from another book about the Kalinago called *Yet We Survive*. The paintings come from this book, too.

If you visit the Carib Territory, you will see a rocky "staircase" coming out of the sea. It is called L'Escalier tête chien – it means "the staircase of the snake" in the Dominican Creole language. This is where, according to the myth, a great snake, known in our story as Bakwa, came out of the sea, slithered on to the land – the rocks are the marks his belly left – and went up to his cave. He will stay there sleeping, as you will read in our story, until the world is at peace.

Many years ago, before man existed,
the Great Spirit created the universe.
There was the **blue** sky above
and the **deep blue** sea below.

Everywhere was peaceful.

Then the Great Spirit created sea creatures: mermaids, octopuses, starfish, and crabs.

These creatures lived undisturbed in the **deep blue** sea.

Among them was a **colossal**, *colourful* snake named Bakwa, the diamond-crested guardian of the Kalinago people.

Bakwa lived far underneath the rocks on the floor of the ocean.

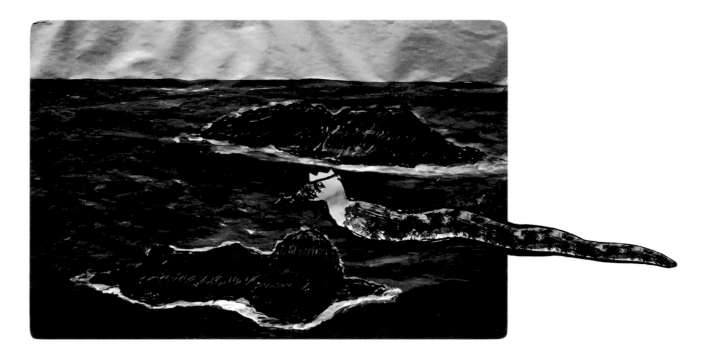

One day, he was no longer comfortable in the sea. He decided to search for a home on land that he could rule over as king.

As Bakwa came out of the sea and slithered over the land, he carved a flight of steps that led to the top of a **very tall** mountain.

When Bakwa got to the top of the mountain and saw the perfectly carved steps, he realised that he had magical powers. At once he **shouted**,

"I am the king of all living creatures on land and in the ocean!"

At the foot of the mountain there was a village called Waraka where the Kalinago people lived in harmony with nature. When they heard Bakwa's voice, they *trembled*.

Among the Kalinago lived a chief named Maruka, who wanted all the good things in life.

One day he decided to visit Bakwa, and travelled many miles through the forest, where many smaller snakes and other wild creatures lived.

13

When Maruka reached the top of a mountain he saw a **huge** cave. At its entrance lay Bakwa with a *magnificent* diamond-crested crown on his head.

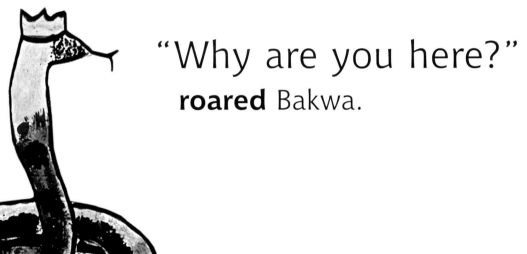

"Why are you here?" **roared** Bakwa.

S haking with fright, Maruka knelt down. He had taken his tobacco pipe with him because he believed it would bring him luck.

He whispered,
"Master I am here
to beg for *three* wishes."

"What do you wish for?"
shouted Bakwa.

"I am a poor and lonely man and wish for my land to supply me with food for many years. I also wish for a *beautiful* wife and children," begged Maruka.

"I will grant you your wishes," said Bakwa, "but in return, I want you to bring me *all* the tobacco that you have grown!"

Maruka returned the following day with *all* the tobacco that he could carry. Bakwa was pleased, and said to Maruka, "Your wishes are granted." Maruka then smoked his pipe with the gr$e$at guardian of his people.

When Maruka went to his garden outside Waraka he saw that his garden was exactly as he had wished!

There were *delicious* fruits such as guava, soursop, pawpaw and pineapple. There were healthy *vegetables* including sweet potato, yam and cassava.

Maruka couldn't wait to share his joy with the other villagers so he ran towards Waraka.

On his way, he met a Kalinago woman named Natari, who was golden in complexion, had eyes as brown as cinnamon and whose hair was the colour of midnight. As soon as he saw her, Maruka fell in love with the beautiful lady.

Maruka married Natari and took her to his house. They had many beautiful children. The world was at peace and they all lived happily for several years.

One day, the villagers saw three **massive** fish on the sea. They were astounded and felt very confused for they had never seen such *strange* fish before!

One man asked, "Are these fish or **gigantic** canoes?"

The villagers saw people come off these canoes,
and went out to them saying,

"Mabrika Mabrika tirirahu!"

This means, "We welcome you with open arms!"

The visitors, who wore lots of clothes and carried long shiny metal objects at their waists, asked for fruits and vegetables, but mostly they wanted land.

The Kalinago people brought them their fruits and vegetables, but Maruka said, "You must ask Bakwa for land. He is the great ruler."

So the visitors went to Bakwa and asked him for land. Bakwa **roared**, "No! I know what you have come to do. You have come to kill me and my people."

T he arguments
led to war.

The Kalinago fought to protect their land
and the *magical* powers of Bakwa.
They used their bows and arrows, but
those weapons were no match for the
guns and swords of their enemies.

After the war, the Kalinago went in to the forest where they were safe because they knew its paths and rivers and its birds and animals well. They planted their gardens and lived happily.

They often saw the forest snakes, who *sang* and *danced* all day helping to protect them.

And Bakwa himself is still sleeping in his cave, and will not wake until the world is at *peace* again.